THIS BOOK BELONGS TO:

_____

Frances Hodgson Burnett
was born in Manchester in 1849.
When she was 16, she and her family
emigrated to America and set up home
in Knoxville, Tennessee. She wrote many
very popular books for children.
One of them, *Little Lord Fauntleroy*,
started a fashion for velvet suits!

———————

Jonathan Mercer's woodcuts have been made
specially for Ladybird Classics. They are individually
hand-crafted from box-wood.

Ladybird books are widely available, but in case of
difficulty may be ordered by post or telephone from:

Ladybird Books – Cash Sales Department
Littlegate Road Paignton Devon TQ3 3BE
Telephone 0803 554761

A catalogue record for this book is available
from the British Library

Published by Ladybird Books Ltd Loughborough Leicestershire UK
Ladybird Books Inc Auburn Maine 04210 USA

LADYBIRD CLASSICS

THE SECRET GARDEN

by Frances Hodgson Burnett

Retold by Joyce Faraday
Illustrated by Gilly Marklew
Woodcuts by Jonathan Mercer

No one liked her at all

MARY LENNOX

Mary Lennox was a spoilt, rude and bad-tempered child. She was never really well, and she was thin, miserable and sour-faced. No one liked her at all.

None of this was really Mary's own fault. She was born in India, where her father worked. He was always busy with his work, and paid no attention to his daughter. Her mother was very pretty, and cared only for parties and pleasure. She left Mary in the care of an Indian nursemaid, who gave the little girl everything she wanted so that she would not cry and upset her mother. So, not surprisingly, Mary grew up into a spoilt and most unpleasant girl.

One hot morning, when Mary was nine years

old, she had a strange feeling that something was wrong. From her room she heard shouts and cries and the patter of hurrying feet, but no one came to her. She lay back on her bed and fell asleep.

When she awoke, the house was silent. Still no one came to her, and she was angry that she had been forgotten. Suddenly the door opened, and two Englishmen came in.

'Why was I forgotten?' Mary asked, stamping her foot. 'Why does nobody come?'

'Poor little kid,' said one of the men. 'There's nobody *left* to come.'

That was how Mary learned that her father and mother had been killed by a disease sweeping the country. The servants had died, too. Mary was alone. There was no one in India to look after her, so she was sent all the way to England to live with her uncle, Mr Craven, at Misselthwaite Manor in Yorkshire.

In London, Mary was met by Mrs Medlock, her uncle's housekeeper. Mary disliked her at once. But then, Mary disliked everyone.

Mrs Medlock thought Mary was a plain, rude child – and she was quite right. As they travelled north, she told Mary about the house. It sounded very grand and gloomy, and stood on the edge of a moor.

'There'll be nothing for you to do, and your uncle won't bother with you,' said Mrs Medlock. 'He's got a crooked back. He was a sour young man until he married. His wife was very pretty, and he worshipped her. When she died, it made him more strange than ever. He's away most of the time, so you'll have to look after yourself.'

It was dark when they got out of the train. A carriage took them to the house, but Mary could see nothing outside in the rainy blackness.

'What's the moor like?' she asked.

'It's just miles and miles of wild land,' replied

A butler opened a huge oak door

Mrs Medlock. 'Nothing grows there but gorse and heather, and nothing lives on it but wild ponies and sheep.'

At last the carriage stopped in a courtyard. A butler opened a huge oak door. 'You're to take her to her room,' he said to Mrs Medlock. 'The Master is going to London tomorrow, and he doesn't want to see her.'

Mary followed Mrs Medlock upstairs and through many corridors to a room with a fire burning and supper on the table.

'This is where you'll live,' Mrs Medlock told Mary. 'Just see you stay here and don't go poking round the rest of the house.'

This was Mary's welcome to Misselthwaite Manor. It made her feel cross and unwanted and lonely.

THE GARDENS

The next morning, Mary awakened to find a housemaid lighting her fire. She was called Martha, and she chatted as she worked.

Mary was not used to friendly servants. In India, she had never said 'Please' or 'Thank you', and once she had slapped her nurse's face when she was angry. Somehow she knew that she must not treat Martha this way. At first Mary had no interest in Martha's chatter, but little by little she began to listen to the friendly Yorkshire voice.

'Eh! You should see all my brothers and sisters in our little cottage on the moor,' Martha said. 'There's twelve of us, and my father only gets sixteen shillings a week. My mother has a job to feed 'em all for that. The fresh air on th' moor makes 'em strong and healthy. Our Dickon, he's twelve, he's always out on th' moor. He's good wi' animals. He's tamed a wild pony.'

When Martha left, Mary went out to play.

'Go and look at the gardens,' Martha had said. 'There's not much growing now, but it's lovely in summer!' She had stopped for a second and then said softly, 'One garden has been shut up for ten years, ever since Mrs Craven died. Mr Craven locked the door and buried the key. He hates that garden.'

The grounds of Misselthwaite Manor were huge. They were divided by high walls, so there were many gardens. In some there were flowers and trees and fountains. Vegetables grew in others. Doors led from one garden to the next, and every garden looked bare and wintry.

Presently an old man came through one of the doors. He had a surly old face and did not seem at all pleased to see Mary.

'I heard a robin in the trees there'

'Can I go through that door?' asked Mary.

'If tha likes,' he replied. 'There's nowt to see.'

Mary was hoping to find the door to the locked garden. She tried many doors, but they all opened easily. There was one wall covered with ivy that seemed to have no door at all. She could see trees behind the wall. A robin on a high branch burst into song. She stopped to listen, and the cheerful notes brought a little smile to her unhappy face. She wandered back to the old man, who ignored her and went on digging.

At last she said, 'There's a garden over there without a door.'

'What garden?' he asked gruffly.

'On the other side of that wall,' she replied. 'I heard a robin in the trees there.'

The old man stood up and a smile spread across his face. Mary saw how much nicer he looked when he smiled. He whistled very softly. The robin landed by the man's foot.

'Here he is,' he said quietly. 'He always comes when I whistle. Isn't he a grand little chap? Look, he knows we're talking about him.' The robin, plump and scarlet-breasted, hopped about, pecking at the earth. Ben Weatherstaff, the gardener, went on digging. 'He's the only friend I've got,' he said. 'When he's not with me, I'm lonely.'

'I'm lonely, too,' said Mary. 'I've never had any friends.'

Ben stopped and looked at her. 'I reckon we're a good bit alike,' he said. 'We're not good-looking and we're as sour as we look.'

Mary had never thought before about her sour face or bad temper. Now that she did, it made her feel uncomfortable. Just then, the robin flew up into a tree and sang with all his voice.

'He's taken a fancy to thee,' said Ben. 'He wants to be your friend.'

Mary looked up at the robin. 'Would you be

14

my friend?' she asked. She spoke softly and kindly, instead of in her usual hard, little voice.

'Why,' said Ben, gently 'tha said that like a real child instead of a sharp old woman. It was nearly like Dickon when he talks to th' wild things on th' moor.'

The robin flew over the wall.

'There *must* be a door to that garden,' Mary said with determination.

'Well, there's none to be found now,' snapped Ben. 'Don't go poking your nose in places where you don't belong.' And he walked off without saying goodbye.

She liked to sit by the fire and talk to Martha

ROBIN SHOWS THE WAY

Mary spent most days out of doors. The cold wind brought a pink glow to her cheeks, and each evening she ate a good meal. After supper, she liked to sit by the fire and talk to Martha.

'Why does Mr Craven hate the locked garden?' Mary asked one evening.

'It was Mrs Craven's garden. She loved it,' Martha said. 'She was sitting on the branch of a tree when it broke and she fell. She was hurt so bad, she died. That's why he hates it. He won't let anyone talk about it.'

Mary had never felt sorry for anyone before, but now she understood how very unhappy Mr Craven must be.

The wind blew across the moor and moaned and roared around the house. Martha called it 'wutherin''. Mary listened, and through the wutherin' she thought she heard a child crying.

'No,' Martha said when Mary asked. 'It's only th' wind or th' scullery maid. She's been cryin' all day with toothache.' And she quickly left the room.

Next day the rain poured down. 'On a day like this at home,' said Martha, 'we all try to keep busy indoors. Except Dickon. He goes out in all weathers. He brought home a fox cub that he found half drowned. He's got a crow, too, called Soot.'

Left on her own, Mary decided to explore the house. She went down corridors and up and down stairs. In the stillness, she heard again the faint sound of a child crying. As she stopped to listen at a door, another door opened and out came Mrs Medlock. 'What are you doing here?'

she demanded. 'Get back to your room at once!'

Mary was angry. She knew that she had heard the cry, and she meant to find out what it was.

The storms passed. 'Wait until th' sun shines on th' golden gorse and th' heather,' said Martha.

'I'd like to see your cottage on the moor, and meet your mother,' said Mary.

'Tha would love my mother,' Martha said. 'She's kind and loving and hard-working. When it's my day out and I can go home to see her, I just jump for joy.'

'I'd like to see Dickon, too,' said Mary.

'Yes, you'd like him,' Martha said. 'Everyone likes Dickon.'

'No one likes me,' said Mary sadly.

'Well, maybe that's because you don't like other people,' said Martha, smiling.

'I never thought of that,' said Mary.

Mary found Ben in the garden. 'Spring's

Suddenly… Mary saw a rusty key

coming,' he said. 'Th' plants are workin' under th' soil. You'll soon see crocuses and daffy-downdillys.'

The robin flew over, and Mary followed him to his perch on the ivy-covered wall. He hopped down onto the soil and, as Mary came nearer, he pecked at the earth for a worm. Suddenly, in the soil, Mary saw a rusty key.

'Perhaps it's the key to the Secret Garden!' she thought, slipping it into her pocket.

After supper, Martha told Mary about her day at home. 'Mother has sent you a present to cheer you up.' She brought out a skipping rope with striped handles and showed Mary how to skip.

'Your mother is very kind,' said Mary, wondering how Martha's mother could have spared the money to buy her a rope. Now, wherever she went, Mary skipped, and the more she skipped, the stronger she grew.

DICKON

One morning, Mary was watching the robin on his perch on the wall, when suddenly something happened that felt like magic! A gust of wind blew the ivy on the wall, and under the leaves Mary saw a door! She felt for the key in her pocket and tried it in the lock. It was very stiff, but she could just turn it. The next second, she was in the Secret Garden!

Mary's heart thumped as she looked round. It was overgrown and untidy, but she thought it was the loveliest place. She saw green shoots of bulbs pushing up through the soil, and she pulled the weeds away to make room for the crocuses and snowdrops. Time slipped by as she went on weeding and clearing dead leaves and grass.

At supper time, she longed to share her secret with Martha, but she dared not in case she should be forbidden to go again to her Secret Garden. Instead, she said, 'I wish I had a bit of a garden to grow things in.'

'That's a lovely idea,' said Martha. 'I'll get Dickon to bring some garden tools and seeds to plant.'

Mary worked with her hands in her Secret Garden every day. She was careful that Ben Weatherstaff never saw where she went. One day Ben said to her, 'This fresh air is doin' thee good. Tha's fatter and not so yeller. Tha looked like a young plucked crow when tha first came.' Mary laughed. She even liked Ben on his grumpy days.

One day Mary saw a boy sitting under a tree. Two rabbits and a pheasant were near him, and a squirrel clung to the tree above his head. They all seemed to be listening to the tune he was playing on a pipe.

She led him through the door

The boy got up slowly, so as not to frighten the animals. His blue eyes smiled from his round, rosy face. 'I'm Dickon,' he said to Mary. 'I've brought tha garden tools and some flower seeds.'

His smile was so gentle and kind that Mary forgot to be shy. She felt that if animals trusted him, she could trust him, too. After a while she asked, 'Do you know about the Secret Garden?'

'I've heard of it,' he said, 'but I don't know where it is.'

Making sure no one was watching, Mary led him through the door in the wall. Dickon was amazed. He looked round at all the plants and trees. 'All these will grow,' he said. 'There'll be flowers and roses everywhere in a few weeks.'

They worked together, weeding and pruning. Mary felt she had never known anyone like Dickon. Trying to speak in a warm, Yorkshire voice like Dickon's and Martha's, she asked, 'Does tha like me?'

'Eh!' he laughed. 'That I does, an' so does the robin.'

After dinner, Mrs Medlock came to take Mary to see Mr Craven. 'He's going away tomorrow, and he wants to see you first,' she said.

Mary felt a little afraid, and very awkward and stiff. But Mr Craven wasn't a bit frightening, nor was his back really crooked. His face was handsome, but looked full of worry and misery. He asked if there was anything she would like. Mary asked for a piece of garden to grow her own flowers.

'Of course,' said her uncle. 'Take any bit that's not being used.' Mary knew which bit this would be. She could call the Secret Garden her own!

COLIN

In the night, Mary was awakened by heavy rain and the wutherin' of the wind. She couldn't sleep, and as she lay tossing in bed, she heard the crying again. 'That's never the wind,' she whispered. 'I don't care what Mrs Medlock says, I'm going to find out what that noise is.'

Candlestick in hand, she walked softly along the corridors. She saw a light shining under a door. She pushed the door open and there, lying on a four-poster bed, she saw a boy crying pitifully.

He turned suddenly and stopped crying. 'Are you a ghost?' he asked, frightened.

'No, I'm Mary Lennox,' she answered. 'Who are you?'

'I must be your cousin,' said Mary

'I'm Mr Craven's son, Colin,' said the boy.

'So I must be your cousin,' said Mary. 'Did no one tell you I'd come to live here?'

'No. No one would dare,' replied Colin. 'I should have been afraid you'd see me. My father won't let people see me. He's afraid I'll grow up to be a hunchback. I'm always ill, so I stay here in bed. My father hates me because my mother died when I was born.'

'Have you always been here?' asked Mary.

'Nearly always,' replied Colin. 'If I go out, people stare at me and I can't stand it.'

'If you don't like people to see you,' Mary said, 'shall I go away?'

'Oh, no!' Colin answered quickly. 'Stay and talk to me.'

Mary sat on a cushioned stool next to the bed, and they talked for a long time. Colin wanted to know all about Mary, and she answered all his questions. He told her how miserable and lonely he felt, even though he was given whatever he asked for.

'All the servants have to please me,' Colin said. 'It makes me ill to be angry, so everyone has to do as I say.'

'Do you think you will get well?' Mary asked.

'I don't suppose I shall,' Colin replied. 'I think I am going to die. But let's talk about something else. How old are you?'

'I'm ten, same as you,' Mary said.

'How do you know I'm ten?' he asked.

'Because the garden was locked ten years ago, when you were born,' Mary answered.

'What garden?' Colin asked, surprised.

'Just a garden Mr Craven hates,' Mary replied. 'He locked the door and buried the key.'

'What's the garden like?' Colin persisted.

'No one has been allowed to see it for ten years,' Mary answered. She was careful not to let him know that she had already found it.

Colin wanted to know all he could about the garden, and they talked about the exciting things they might find there.

'I shall make them open the door,' Colin said.

'Oh, no!' cried Mary. 'Let's keep it a secret. If they open the door, it will never be a secret again. Perhaps one day we may find the door. We could go inside, and no one would know about it but us.'

'I should like that,' said Colin. 'I never had a secret before.' Tired from talking, he fell asleep, and Mary crept away.

Mary told Martha about the crying

RAINY DAYS

The next morning, Mary told Martha about the crying and how she had found Colin. Poor Martha was very upset. She thought she might lose her job for allowing Mary to find the young master of the house.

'You needn't worry,' Mary told her. 'Colin was pleased, and he wants to see me every day.'

'Tha must have bewitched him!' Martha cried.

'What's the matter with him?' Mary asked.

Martha told her that since he was born, Colin had not been allowed to walk. His father thought his back was weak. A famous doctor had been to see him, and had said he would get strong if less fuss was made of him. But still he was spoiled and given his own way.

33

'Colin thinks he will die,' said Mary. 'Do you think so?'

'Mother says there's no reason for a child to live if he can't get out in the fresh air,' Martha replied.

'It's done me good to be outside,' said Mary. 'Do you think it would help Colin?'

'Eh! I don't know,' Martha said. 'He had a bad tantrum when he was taken into the garden. He got angry because he thought one of the gardeners was looking at him. He cried so much he was ill all night.'

'Well,' said Mary, 'if he ever gets angry with me, I shan't go to see him again.'

On her next visit to Colin, Mary told him about Dickon. 'He's not like anyone else,' she said. 'He can charm the animals on the moor. When he plays his pipe, they come to listen.'

'The moor sounds a wonderful place,' said Colin, 'but I'll never see it. I'm going to die.'

'How do you know?' Mary asked, feeling a little cross. Colin talked about dying almost as though it pleased him.

'Everyone says I will,' Colin replied. 'I think my father will be glad when I'm not here.'

'I don't believe that,' said Mary. 'That famous doctor was right. They should make less fuss of you, and they should let you go out. If you could only see Dickon, you'd want to get well!' And she told him all about Dickon's family, who were so well and happy even though they were so poor.

It rained for a week, so Mary could not visit the garden. Instead, she spent her days with Colin. They read and talked and, for the first time, Colin started to laugh. He often spoke of the garden and what might be in it. Mary longed to share her secret with him, but felt that she could not yet trust him.

Mary was breathless with happiness

THE SECRET IS TOLD

After the rain, Mary awoke early one
morning to find the sun streaming through the
blinds. When she ran down to the Secret Garden,
she found that Dickon was already there.

'I couldn't stay in bed on a morning like this,'
he cried. 'Look at th' garden!' The rain and the
warmth had made all the new shoots push up
through the earth. There were clumps of orange
and purple crocuses. Mary was breathless with
happiness.

The robin was building a nest. 'We mustn't
watch too close,' warned Dickon. 'He's too busy
now for visitin' an' gossipin'.'

A whole week had passed since Mary had last
seen Dickon. She told him about finding Colin.

'If we could get him out here,' said Dickon, 'he'd forget about lumps growing on his back. We'd be just two lads and a little lass lookin' on at th' springtime. It'd do him more good than doctor's stuff.'

When Mary went in at the end of the day, Martha told her that Colin was angry because she had not been to see him.

'I won't let that boy come if you stay with him instead of me!' Colin raged when Mary went to see him. 'You're selfish for not coming!'

'What are *you?*' snapped Mary. 'You're the most selfish person I know!'

'Well, I'm going to die!' wailed Colin.

'I don't believe it,' said Mary sourly. 'You only want people to be sorry for you. But they're not! You're too nasty!' She marched to the door and called back, 'I was going to tell you about Dickon and his fox and crow, but I shan't now.' And she shut the door firmly behind her.

Later, as she thought of Colin's lonely day, her anger faded and she felt sorry for him. 'If he wants to see me tomorrow,' she thought, 'I'll go and sit with him.'

In the night, Mary was awakened by noises in the corridor, and she could hear sobbing and screaming. 'It's Colin having a tantrum,' she thought. She covered her ears, but she couldn't shut out the dreadful sounds.

She jumped out of bed and stamped her foot angrily. 'Somebody must stop him,' she cried. 'He deserves a beating for being so selfish! He's upsetting everyone in the house!' She ran into Colin's room and shouted, 'Stop! I hate you! You'll scream yourself to death in a minute, and I wish you would!'

Colin looked dreadful. His face was swollen and he was gasping and choking, but Mary was too angry to care. 'If you scream again, I shall scream louder!' she stormed.

She looked carefully at the poor, thin back

'I can't stop,' sobbed Colin. 'I've felt a lump coming on my back!'

'Turn over and let me look,' Mary ordered. She looked carefully at the poor, thin back. 'There's not a lump as big as a pin,' she announced. 'Don't you ever talk about it again!'

Colin's sobbing slowly died, and Mary sat by his bed quietly comforting him until he fell asleep.

In the morning Mary found Dickon in the garden with his squirrels, and she told him of Colin's sobbing in the night.

'Eh! We mun get him out here, poor lad,' said Dickon.

'Aye, that we mun,' said Mary, using the same Yorkshire words.

Dickon laughed. 'Tha mun talk a bit o' Yorkshire to Colin,' he said. 'It'll make him laugh, and Mother says laughing's good for ill folk.'

When Mary went to see Colin, she told him

about Dickon and his squirrels, Nut and Shell. They laughed and talked for a long time. Then Colin said, 'I'm sorry that I said I'd send Dickon away. I didn't mean it. He sounds like a wonderful boy.'

'I'm glad you said that,' said Mary, 'because he's coming to see you, and he's bringing his animals.'

Colin cheered up. He looked so happy that Mary suddenly decided to take a chance.

'That's not all,' she said. 'There's something better. I've found the door to the garden!'

Colin was overjoyed. 'Then shall we go in and find out what's inside?' he asked.

Mary paused – and then boldly told the truth. 'I've already been in it. That's why I could tell you so much about it. I didn't dare tell you my secret until I was sure I could trust you.'

'I SHALL LIVE
FOR EVER AND EVER!'

At breakfast, Colin announced to his nurse, 'A boy and some animals are coming to see me. Bring them straight up when they arrive.'

It wasn't long before Mary heard a bleating. 'That's Dickon's lamb!' she cried. 'They're coming!'

Dickon came in smiling. He carried a lamb, and his little fox trotted beside him. Nut the squirrel sat on one shoulder and Soot the crow on the other. His other squirrel, Shell, peeped out of a pocket.

Colin stared in wonder. Dickon gently put the lamb in Colin's lap and gave him a bottle to feed it. They were all so busy and happy together.

43

The whole world changed for Colin

'I'm going to see it all!' cried Colin.

'Aye, that tha mun,' said Mary, 'an' tha munnot lose no time about it.'

Colin was put in his chair, and Dickon pushed it along the paths. As they went, Mary told Colin about the places they passed. 'Here's where I met Ben,' she said, 'and this is where I saw the robin. And this,' she whispered, 'this is the garden!'

Mary opened the door, and Dickon pushed the chair inside quickly. Colin looked round for a long time, seeing all the things Mary had described. Then he cried out, 'I shall get well! I shall live for ever and ever!' That afternoon, the whole world changed for Colin.

'It's been a grand day,' said Dickon.

'Aye, that it has,' said Mary.

'Does tha think,' said Colin, 'that it was made like this 'ere all for me?'

'My word!' said Mary. 'That's a good bit of

Yorkshire!' And they all joined in the laughter.

'I don't want this day to go,' said Colin, 'but I shall come back every day.'

'That tha will,' said Dickon, 'an' we shall soon have thee digging and walking.'

Suddenly Ben Weatherstaff's face glared down at them from the top of the wall. 'What are you doing in there?' he shouted at Mary. Then he saw Colin, and his mouth opened in surprise.

'Do you know who I am?' Colin asked.

'Aye, that I do,' Ben answered. 'Th'art th' poor cripple lad.'

Colin sat up angrily. 'I'm not a cripple! I'll show you!' he cried. He struggled out of the chair and with Dickon's help, stood straight and tall. 'Look at me now!' he shouted.

'God bless thee, lad!' said Ben, and tears ran down his face.

Colin remained standing. He suddenly felt his fear leave him. 'I'm not afraid any more!' he cried. 'It's the Magic of the Secret Garden! It's working to make all the plants grow, and it will work for me.'

That evening Colin was quiet. After a long time, he said to Mary, 'I'm not going to be a poor thing any more. If I believe I shall get strong and well, the Magic will make it happen.'

MAGIC

Next day in the garden, Colin called Mary, Dickon and Ben to him. 'I'm going to show you that the Magic works,' he said.

Slowly, taking a few steps at a time, Colin walked right round the garden. His face was flushed with joy.

'This must be the biggest secret of all,' he said. 'When I can walk and run well, I shall walk into my father's study and say, "Here I am, well and strong!"'

It was very hard to keep the secret. The Magic of the Secret Garden was making Colin bright-eyed and rosy-cheeked. Each day Colin and Mary did exercises to make them strong, and they both grew plumper and healthier. Mary became pretty, and Colin no longer looked like an invalid. Everyone was amazed at the change.

Now, while the Secret Garden was working its Magic, Mr Craven was travelling in faraway places. For ten years he had been trying to run away from his sorrow and had refused to be comforted.

Then one day, whilst walking in Austria, he sat down by a stream. Gradually he felt his mind and body relax. The peace of the place filled him, and from that moment he felt healthier and happier.

One night, he dreamt of his wife's garden at Misselthwaite Manor. The dream was so clear that he decided to return home at once. As soon as he arrived home, he went to the garden.

He walked slowly, as all his sad memories came rushing back. As he stood by the door of the Secret Garden, wondering how to find the key, he heard laughter coming from the other side of the wall.

'Father, I'm Colin'

Suddenly the door burst open and a boy ran out, almost into his arms. He was a tall, handsome boy, and Mr Craven gazed at him, unable to speak.

Colin stood still and recovered his breath. Then he said, 'Father, I'm Colin. You can't believe it, but it's true.'

He led his father into the garden and told him how the Magic had made everything grow, and had made him strong and well.

Mr Craven had never heard such a wonderful story. He sat by Mary and Dickon and the animals and laughed as he had not done for years. He was so proud of his handsome, healthy son!

'Now,' said Colin, 'it needn't be a secret any more. I shall never need my chair again. I shall walk with you, Father!'

They stood up and walked towards the house. At Mr Craven's side, strong and straight as any lad in Yorkshire, walked his son.